# Lily and B[illegible]r

D0334914

Lisa Stubbs

Boxer Books

Lily loved to draw.
She drew
cats and girls,
birds and boats,
and houses
and hearts.

She drew the sea
and a pirate ship
and a teapot.

She drew tricycles
and a banjo.

And then she drew . . .

Bear.

Lily loved Bear and Bear loved Lily.

Lily took Bear by the paw . . .

They attended royal tea parties

and sailed carpet seas.

They did Lily's favourite thing
and drew BIG pictures.

Then they raced
around on tricycles.

But best of all,
they sang really
loudly while
Bear played
the banjo
brilliantly.

Lily loved Bear and Bear loved Lily.

After a while, Bear sat down.

He didn't want to attend royal tea parties, sail pirate ships or ride tricycles any more. Bear wanted to do Bear things.

Lily loved Bear
and Bear loved Lily
so Bear took Lily
by the hand . . .

They picked
huckleberries,
and ate them
from Bear's paws.

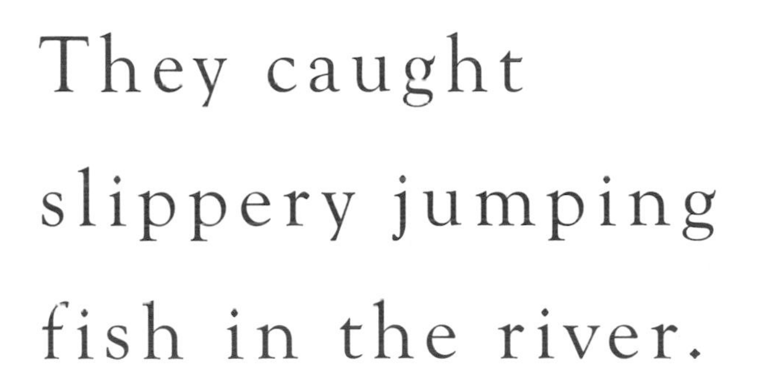

They caught
slippery jumping
fish in the river.

They did Bear's
favourite thing
and scratched
their backs on
a knotty pine.

Then
they rolled
down the
mountainside.

But best of all, as the stars started to shine, they sang a really quiet song while Bear gently played the banjo brilliantly until . . .

. . . it was time to
sleep and dream of
their next adventure.

"I love you, Bear."
"And I love you, Lily."